THE CAT IN THE HAT

By Dr. Seuss

The sun did not shine.

It was too wet to play.

So we sat in the house

All that cold, cold, wet day.

I sat there with Sally.

We sat there, we two.

And I said, "How I wish

We had something to do!"

Too wet to go out

And too cold to play ball.

So we sat in the house.

We did nothing at all.

So all we could do was to
Sit!
    Sit!
        Sit!
            Sit!
And we did not like it.
Not one little bit.

And then
Something went BUMP!
How that bump made us jump!

We looked!

Then we saw him step in on the mat!

We looked!

And we saw him!

The Cat in the Hat!

And he said to us,

"Why do you sit there like that?"

"I know it is wet

And the sun is not sunny.

But we can have

Lots of good fun that is funny!"

"I know some good games we could play,"
Said the cat.

"I know some new tricks,"
Said the Cat in the Hat.

"A lot of good tricks.
I will show them to you.
Your mother
Will not mind at all if I do."

Then Sally and I
Did not know what to say.
Our mother was out of the house
For the day.

But our fish said, "No! No!

Make that cat go away!

Tell that Cat in the Hat

You do NOT want to play.

He should not be here.

He should not be about.

He should not be here

When your mother is out!"

"Now! Now! Have no fear.
Have no fear!" said the cat.
"My tricks are not bad,"
Said the Cat in the Hat.
"Why, we can have
Lots of good fun, if you wish,
With a game that I call
Up-up-up with a fish!"

"Put me down!" said the fish.
"This is no fun at all!
Put me down!" said the fish.
"I do NOT wish to fall!"

"Have no fear!" said the cat.

"I will not let you fall.

I will hold you up high

As I stand on a ball.

With a book on one hand!

And a cup on my hat!

But that is not ALL I can do!"

Said the cat . . .

"Look at me!

Look at me now!" said the cat.

"With a cup and a cake

On the top of my hat!

I can hold up TWO books!

I can hold up the fish!

And a little toy ship!

And some milk on a dish!

And look!

I can hop up and down on the ball!

But that is not all!

Oh, no.

That is not all . . .

"Look at me!

Look at me!

Look at me NOW!

It is fun to have fun

But you have to know how.

I can hold up the cup

And the milk and the cake!

I can hold up these books!

And the fish on a rake!

I can hold the toy ship

And a little toy man!

And look! With my tail

I can hold a red fan!

I can fan with the fan

As I hop on the ball!

But that is not all.

Oh, no.

That is not all. . . ."

That is what the cat said . . .

Then he fell on his head!

He came down with a bump

From up there on the ball.

And Sally and I,

We saw ALL the things fall!

And our fish came down, too.

He fell into a pot!

He said, "Do I like this?

Oh, no! I do not.

This is not a good game,"

Said our fish as he lit.

"No, I do not like it,

Not one little bit!"

"Now look what you did!"

Said the fish to the cat.

"Now look at this house!

Look at this! Look at that!

You sank our toy ship,

Sank it deep in the cake.

You shook up our house

And you bent our new rake

You SHOULD NOT be here

When our mother is not.

You get out of this house!"

Said the fish in the pot.

"But I like to be here.
Oh, I like it a lot!"
Said the Cat in the Hat
To the fish in the pot.
"I will NOT go away.
I do NOT wish to go!
And so," said the Cat in the Hat,
"So

    so

      so . . .

I will show you
Another good game that I know!"

And then he ran out.

And, then, fast as a fox,

The Cat in the Hat

Came back in with a box.

A big red wood box.

It was shut with a hook.

"Now look at this trick,"

Said the cat.

"Take a look!"

Then he got up on top

With a tip of his hat.

"I call this game FUN-IN-A-BOX,"

Said the cat.

"In this box are two things

I will show to you now.

You will like these two things,"

Said the cat with a bow.

"I will pick up the hook.

You will see something new.

Two things. And I call them

Thing One and Thing Two.

These Things will not bite you.

They want to have fun."

Then, out of the box

Came Thing Two and Thing One!

And they ran to us fast.

They said, "How do you do?

Would you like to shake hands

With Thing One and Thing Two?"

And Sally and I

Did not know what to do.

So we had to shake hands

With Thing One and Thing Two.

We shook their two hands.

But our fish said, "No! No!

Those Things should not be

In this house! Make them go!

"They should not be here
When your mother is not!
Put them out! Put them out!"
Said the fish in the pot.

"Have no fear, little fish,"
Said the Cat in the Hat.
"These Things are good Things."
And he gave them a pat.
"They are tame. Oh, so tame!
They have come here to play.
They will give you some fun
On this wet, wet, wet day."

"Now, here is a game that they like,"
Said the cat.
"They like to fly kites,"
Said the Cat in the Hat.

"No! Not in the house!"

Said the fish in the pot.

"They should not fly kites

In a house! They should not.

Oh, the things they will bump!

Oh, the things they will hit!

Oh, I do not like it!

Not one little bit!"

Then Sally and I
Saw them run down the hall.
We saw those two Things
Bump their kites on the wall!
Bump! Thump! Thump! Bump!
Down the wall in the hall.

Thing Two and Thing One!

They ran up! They ran down!

On the string of one kite

We saw Mother's new gown!

Her gown with the dots

That are pink, white and red.

Then we saw one kite bump

On the head of her bed!

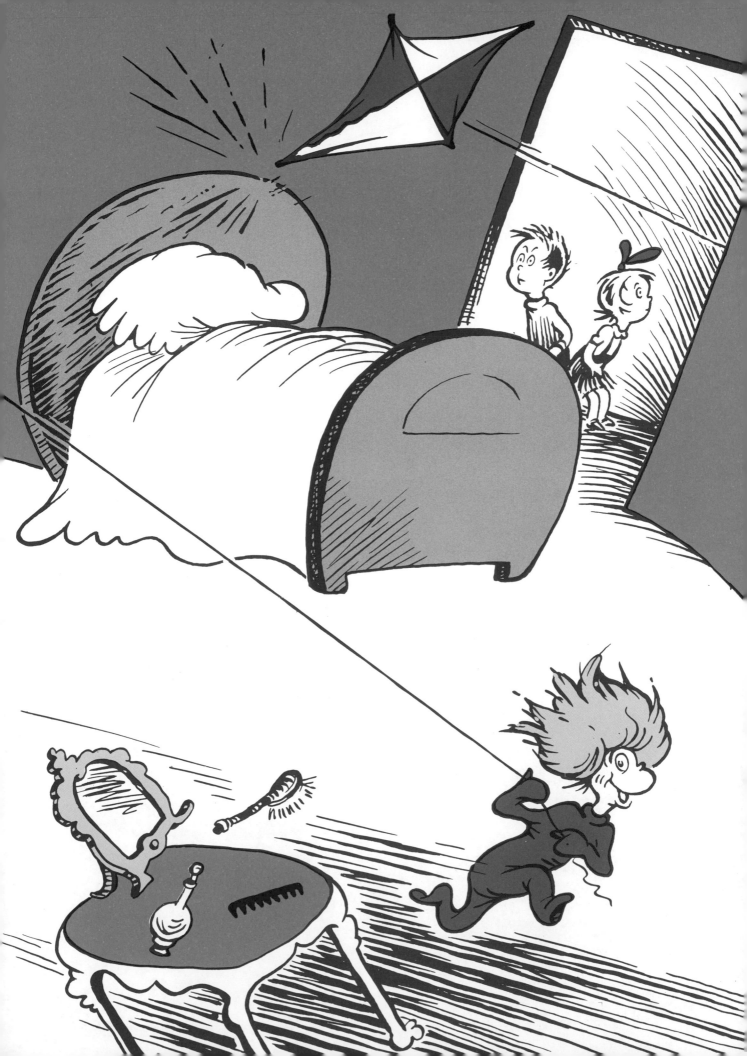

Then those Things ran about

With big bumps, jumps and kicks

And with hops and big thumps

And all kinds of bad tricks.

And I said,

"I do NOT like the way that they play!

If Mother could see this,

Oh, what would she say!"

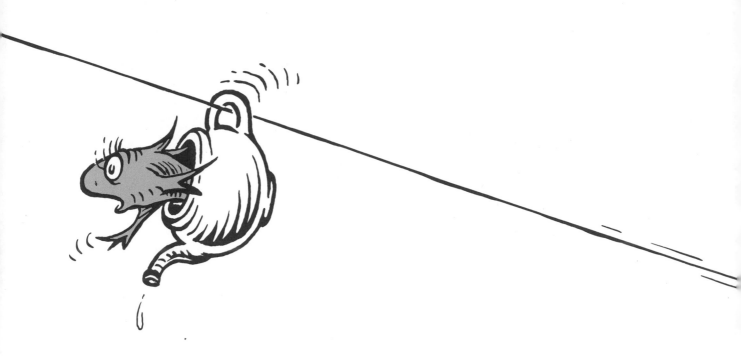

Then our fish said, "LOOK! LOOK!"

And our fish shook with fear.

"Your mother is on her way home!

Do you hear?

Oh, what will she do to us?

What will she say?

Oh, she will not like it

To find us this way!"

"So, DO something! Fast!" said the fish.

"Do you hear!

I saw her. Your mother!

Your mother is near!

So, as fast as you can,

Think of something to do!

You will have to get rid of

Thing One and Thing Two!"

So, as fast as I could,

I went after my net.

And I said, "With my net

I can get them I bet.

I bet, with my net,

I can get those Things yet!"

Then I let down my net.

It came down with a PLOP!

And I had them! At last!

Those two Things had to stop.

Then I said to the cat,

"Now you do as I say.

You pack up those Things

And you take them away!"

"Oh dear!" said the cat.

"You did not like our game . . .

Oh dear.

What a shame!

What a shame!

What a shame!"

Then he shut up the Things

In the box with the hook.

And the cat went away

With a sad kind of look.

"That is good," said the fish.

"He has gone away. Yes.

But your mother will come.

She will find this big mess!

And this mess is so big

And so deep and so tall,

We can not pick it up.

There is no way at all!"

And THEN!

Who was back in the house?

Why, the cat!

"Have no fear of this mess,"

Said the Cat in the Hat.

"I always pick up all my playthings

And so . . .

I will show you another

Good trick that I know!"

Then we saw him pick up

All the things that were down.

He picked up the cake,

And the rake, and the gown,

And the milk, and the strings,

And the books, and the dish,

And the fan, and the cup,

And the ship, and the fish.

And he put them away.

Then he said, "That is that."

And then he was gone

With a tip of his hat.

Then our mother came in
And she said to us two,
"Did you have any fun?
Tell me. What did you do?"

And Sally and I did not know
What to say.
Should we tell her
The things that went on there that day?

Should we tell her about it?

Now, what SHOULD we do?

Well ...

What would YOU do

If your mother asked YOU?

THE CAT IN THE HAT COMES BACK

By Dr. Seuss

This was no time for play.
This was no time for fun.
This was no time for games.
There was work to be done.

All that deep,

Deep, deep snow,

All that snow had to go.

When our mother went
Down to the town for the day,
She said, "Somebody has to
Clean all this away.
Somebody, SOMEBODY
Has to, you see."
Then she picked out two Somebodies.
Sally and me.

Well . . .

There we were.

We were working like that

And then who should come up

But the CAT IN THE HAT!

"Oh-oh!" Sally said.

"Don't you talk to that cat.

That cat is a bad one,

That Cat in the Hat.

He plays lots of bad tricks.

Don't you let him come near.

You know what he did

The last time he was here."

"Play tricks?" laughed the cat.
"Oh, my my! No, no, no!
I just want to go in
To get out of the snow.
Keep your mind on your work.
You just stay there, you two.
I will go in the house
And find something to do."

Then that cat went right in!

He was up to no good!

So I ran in after

As fast as I could!

Do you know where I found him?

You know where he was?

He was eating a cake in the tub!

Yes he was!

The hot water was on

And the cold water, too.

And I said to the cat,

"What a bad thing to do!"

"But I like to eat cake

In a tub," laughed the cat.

"You should try it some time,"

Laughed the cat as he sat.

And then I got mad.

This was no time for fun.

I said, "Cat! You get out!

There is work to be done.

I have no time for tricks.

I must go back and dig.

I can't have you in here

Eating cake like a pig!

You get out of this house!

We don't want you about!"

Then I shut off the water

And let it run out.

The water ran out.

And then I SAW THE RING!

A ring in the tub!

And, oh boy! What a thing!

A big long pink cat ring!

It looked like pink ink!

And I said, "Will this ever

Come off? I don't think!"

"Have no fear of that ring,"
Laughed the Cat in the Hat.
"Why, I can take cat rings
Off tubs. Just like that!"

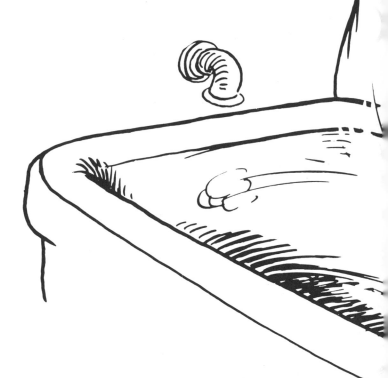

Do you know how he did it?
WITH MOTHER'S WHITE DRESS!
Now the tub was all clean,
But her dress was a mess!

Then Sally looked in.

Sally saw the dress, too!

And Sally and I

Did not know what to do.

We should work in the snow.

But that dress! What a spot!

"It may never come off!"

Sally said. "It may not!"

But the cat laughed, "Ho! Ho!
I can make the spot go.
The way I take spots off a dress
Is just so!"

"See here!" laughed the cat.

"It is not hard at all.

The thing that takes spots

Off a dress is a wall!"

Then we saw the cat wipe

The spot off the dress.

Now the dress was all clean.

But the wall! What a mess!

"Oh, wall spots!" he laughed.
"Let me tell you some news.
To take spots off a wall,
All I need is two shoes!"

Whose shoes did he use?
I looked and saw whose!
And I said to the cat,
"This is very bad news.
Now the spot is all over
DAD'S £7 SHOES!"

"But your dad will not
Know about that,"
Said the cat.
"He will never find out,"
Laughed the Cat in the Hat.
"His £7 shoes will have
No spots at all.
I will rub them right off
On this rug in the hall."

"But now we have rug spots!"
I yelled. "What a day!
Rug spots! What next?
Can you take THEM away?"

"Don't ask me," he laughed.
"Why, you know that I can!"
Then he picked up the rug
And away the cat ran.

"I can clean up these rug spots
Before you count three!
No spots are too hard
For a Hat Cat like me!"

He ran into Dad's bedroom
And then the cat said,
"It is good that your dad
Has the right kind of bed."

Then he shook the rug!

CRACK!

Now the bed had the spot!

And all I could say was,

"Now what, Cat?

NOW what?"

But the cat just stood still.

He just looked at the bed.

"This is NOT the right kind of a bed,"

The cat said.

"To take spots off THIS bed

Will be hard," said the cat.

"I can't do it alone,"

Said the Cat in the Hat.

"It is good I have some one
To help me," he said.
"Right here in my hat
On the top of my head!
It is good that I have him
Here with me today.
He helps me a lot.
This is Little Cat A."

And then Little Cat A
Took the hat off HIS head.
"It is good I have some one
To help ME," he said.
"This is Little Cat B.
And I keep him about,
And when I need help
Then I let him come out."

And then B said,

"I think we need Little Cat C.

That spot is too much

For the A cat and me.

But now, have no fear!

We will clean it away!

The three of us! Little Cats B, C and A!"

"Come on! Take it away!"
Yelled Little Cat A.

"I will hit that old spot
With this broom! Do you see?
It comes off the old bed!
It goes on the T.V."

And then Little Cat B
Cleaned up the T.V.

He cleaned it with milk,
Put the spot in a pan!
And then C blew it out
Of the house with a fan!

"But look where it went!"
I said. "Look where it blew!
You blew the mess
Out of the house. That is true.
But now you made Snow Spots!
You can't let THEM stay!"

"Let us think about that now,"
Said C, B and A.

"With some help, we can do it!"
Said Little Cat C.
Then POP! On his head
We saw Little Cat D!
Then, POP! POP! POP!
Little Cats E, F and G!

"We will clean up that snow
If it takes us all day!
If it takes us all night,
We will clean it away!"
Said Little Cats G, F, E, D, C, B, A.

They ran out of the house then

And we ran out, too.

And the Big Cat laughed,

"Now you will see something new!

My cats are all clever.

My cats are good shots.

My cats have good guns.

They will kill all those spots!"

But this did not look
Very clever to me.
Kill snow spots with pop guns?
That just could not be!

"All this does is make MORE spots!"

We yelled at the cat.

"Your cats are no good.

Put them back in your hat.

"Take your Little Cats G,
F, E, D, C, B, A.
Put them back in your hat
And you take them away!"

"Oh, no!" said the cat.
"All they need is more help.
Help is all that they need.
So keep still and don't yelp."

Then Little Cat G
Took the hat off his head.
"I have Little Cat H
Here to help us," he said.

"Little Cats H, I, J,

K, L and M.

But our work is so hard

We must have more than them.

We need Little Cat N.

We need O. We need P.

We need Little Cats Q, R, S, T,

U and V."

"Come on! Kill those spots!
Kill the mess!" yelled the cats.
And they jumped at the snow
With long rakes and red bats.
They put it in pails
And they made high pink hills!
Pink snow men! Pink snow balls!
And little pink pills!

Oh, the things that they did!
And they did them so hard,
It was all one big spot now
All over the yard!
But the Big Cat stood there
And he said, "This is good.
This is what they should do
And I knew that they would.

"With a little more help,
All the work will be done.
They need one more cat.
And I know just the one."

"Look close! In my hand
I have Little Cat V.
On his head are Cats W,
X, Y and Z."

"Z is too small to see.

So don't try. You can not.

But Z is the cat

Who will clean up that spot!"

"Now here is the Z
You can't see," said the Cat.
"And I bet you can't guess
What he has in HIS hat!

"He has something called VOOM.

Voom is so hard to get,

You never saw anything

Like it, I bet.

Why, Voom cleans up anything

Clean as can be!"

Then he yelled,

"Take your hat off now,

Little Cat Z!

Take the Voom off your head!

Make it clean up the snow!

Hurry! You Little Cat!

One! Two! Three! GO!"

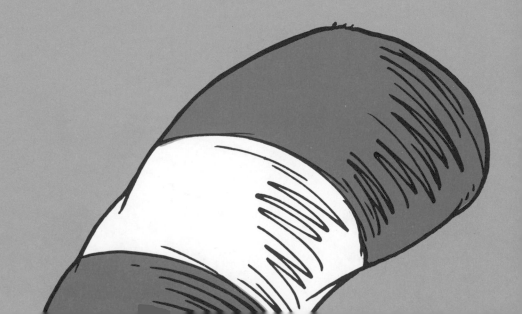

Then the Voom . . .

It went VOOM!

And, oh boy! What a VOOM!

Now, don't ask me what Voom is.

I never will know.

But, boy! Let me tell you

It DOES clean up snow!

"So you see!" laughed the Cat,

"Now your snow is all white!

Now your work is all done!

Now your house is all right!

And you know where my little cats are?"

Said the cat.

"That Voom blew my little cats

Back in my hat.

And so, if you ever

Have spots, now and then,

I will be very happy

To come here again . . .

"... with Little Cats A, B, C, D ...

E, F, G ...

H, I, J, K ...

L, M, N ...

and O, P . .

. and Q, R, S, T . . .

and Cat U and Cat V . . .

and Little Cats W

X

Y

and Z!"

The Complete Cat in the Hat

This omnibus edition first published 2002
by HarperCollins*Children's Books*,
a division of HarperCollins*Publishers* Ltd
77-85 Fulham Palace Road, London W6 8JB

Printed and bound in Spain